For Diarmid, my wee bundle
of choice and wisdom

Nancy Paulsen Books
an imprint of Penguin Random House LLC
Visit us at penguinrandomhouse.com

Nancy Paulsen Books is a registered trademark of Penguin Random House LLC.

Library of Congress Cataloging-in-Publication Data is available upon request.

Manufactured in China by RR Donnelley Asia Printing Solutions Ltd.
ISBN 9780399544460
Special Markets ISBN 9780593111727 Not for Resale
1 3 5 7 9 10 8 6 4 2

Design by Marikka Tamura.
Text hand-lettered by Cinders McLeod.
The illustrations were drawn with HB pencil on Mylar film
and then digitally colored.

This Imagination Library edition is published by Penguin Young Readers, a division
of Penguin Random House, exclusively for Dolly Parton's Imagination Library,
a not-for-profit program designed to inspire a love of reading and learning, sponsored
in part by The Dollywood Foundation. Penguin's trade editions of this work are
available wherever books are sold.

This is ← Sonny.

This is → Sonny's mom.

And this is Sonny's allowance jar. This is where ← he keeps his carrots.

SPEND

Carrots are money in Bunnyland.

Every Saturday,
Sonny gets 3 carrots
for his allowance.

Sonny LOVES Saturdays.

I want to buy

When I see a
bouncy castle
I want to BUY it!

One problem, Sonny.
You only get 3 carrots a week
for allowance,
so you can't buy
everything.

But I
WANT
everything!

Well,
you are going
to have to choose.
Making a choice
helps you see
what's really
important
to you.

Choosing is hard!

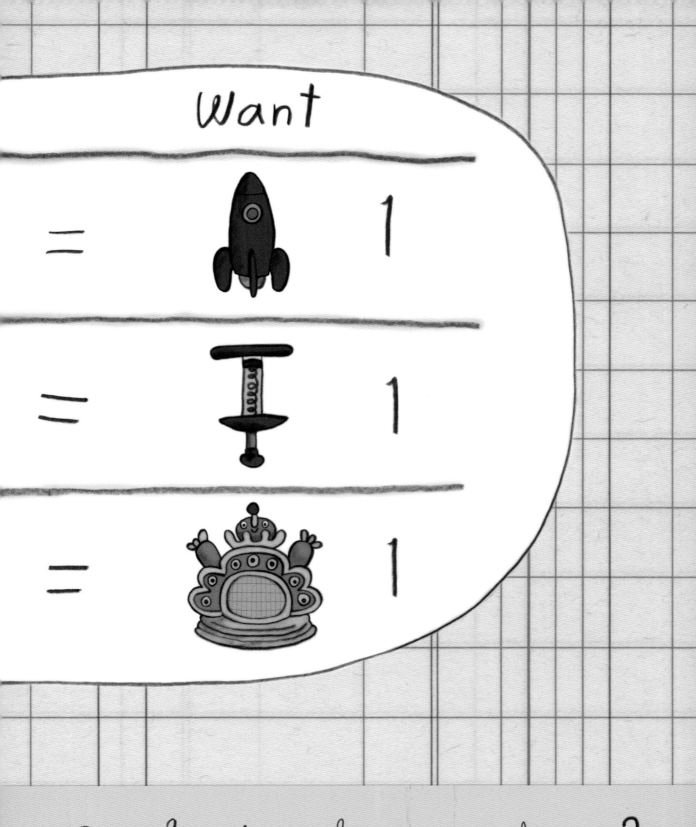

So why do I have to choose?

Because the things you want
don't all cost the same amount.
So let's give this more thought.

Well, let's see.
You really like
that toy rocket?

I
LOVE
it !

Okay. That toy rocket costs 2 carrots.

And you really like that pogo stick?

I LOVE it!

Okay. That pogo stick costs 3 carrots.

The bouncy castle costs

100 carrots.

That's RIDICULOUS!

Well —
it's not ridiculous
if you have
100 carrots
and
nothing else
to spend
it on.

STILL ridiculous!
Forget the bouncy castle.

And the toy? You already have lots of toys.

Yeah. Forget the toy. Hmmm, what CAN I buy with my 3 carrots?

POGO STICK!

Great!
Sounds like you
made your choice.
How about
we go to
the toy store
now...

Wow, Sonny! You're getting good
at this money stuff.

Boing, boing, boing.

The end

The Moneybunny Books...

...are a series of books for young children to help teach them a few simple facts about money.

In EARN IT! talented Bun wants to be RICH and FAMOUS but learns that it takes work.
In SPEND IT! enthusiastic Sonny wants to BUY EVERYTHING but learns to make choices.

Do they get what they want?
Not exactly!
Do they discover something more valuable?
Yes!

It's never too early to teach your little bunny about money!

And watch for:
SAVE IT!
GIVE IT!